T0204919

STRANGE WATER

1366Bᴏᴏks

Guernica Editions Inc. acknowledges the support of
the Canada Council for the Arts and the Ontario Arts Council.
The Ontario Arts Council is an agency of the Government of Ontario.

We acknowledge the financial support of the Government of Canada.

STRANGE WATER

SARAH MOSES

1366Books

An imprint of Guernica Editions

TORONTO—CHICAGO—BUFFALO—LANCASTER (U.K.)

2024

Copyright © 2024, Sarah Moses and Guernica Editions Inc.
All rights reserved. The use of any part of this publication, reproduced, transmitted in any form or by any means, electronic, mechanical, photocopying, recording or otherwise stored in a retrieval system, without the prior consent of the publisher is an infringement of the copyright law.

Guernica founder: Antonio D'Alfonso
General editor: Michael Mirolla
1366 Books editor: Stuart Ross
Interior design & typesetting: Stuart Ross
Cover & 1366 logo design: Underline Studio
Author photo: Javier Ramallo

Guernica Editions Inc.
1241 Marble Rock Rd., Gananoque, ON K7G 2V4
2250 Military Road, Tonawanda, NY 14150-6000 USA
www.guernicaeditions.com

Distributors:
Independent Publishers Group (IPG), 600 North Pulaski Rd., Chicago IL 60624
University of Toronto Press Distribution (UTP), 5201 Dufferin St., Toronto Ontario M3H 5T8

First edition. Printed in Canada.
Legal Deposit—Third Quarter

Library and Archives Canada Cataloguing in Publication

Title: Strange water / Sarah Moses.
Names: Moses, Sarah, author.
Description: Series statement: 1366 Books ; 2
Identifiers: Canadiana (print) 20240389050 | Canadiana (ebook) 20240389123 | ISBN 9781771839136
(softcover) | ISBN 9781771839143 (EPUB)
Subjects: LCGFT: Short stories.
Classification: LCC PS8626.O84255 S77 2024 | DDC C813/.6—dc23

CONTENTS

STRANGE ANGER

At dawn, my neighbours' dinner is on my lawn.

My neighbours are in their apartment, washing their faces and brushing their teeth. Their apartment is one floor above mine, their dinner outside mine, attracting flies and cockroaches. The flies and cockroaches are atop the two fatty steaks, the burned onions, the squeezed lemons.

The sun is orange when it rises. It sneaks between the leaves, and the steaks begin to steam. All morning, and late into the afternoon, the garden smells of barbecuing meat.

In the evening, my neighbours come home from work. They turn on the radio and loll along. Outside, the sky turns blue.

My neighbours open their windows and turn on the oven. As the heat lifts off the lit-up city, smoke from cooked meat fills the garden again.

They carry forks and knives, glasses and plates to the balcony. They set the table and sit down around it. They have a good chat. It becomes a heated chat. There are shouts of strange anger.

Silhouettes of my neighbours' neighbours appear in windows. We wave hello.

Then it begins. We look on as beef patties, French fries, and a salt shaker shaped like a cow sail over the railing.

NOTHING IS REQUIRED OF YOU

Well, maybe a few things. Good neighbourliness, for example. By this I
mean that you take care of the fairy ring and webbing on your property.
That you take care not to throw household items, such as spatulas or other
kitchen implements, on mine. Take care of your front porch and your
gutters, especially after a downpour, especially in early June, when the
downpours are frequent and forceful. The hedges—don't forget to trim
them. Make sure to keep your budgerigars well fed and in good spirits.
If you borrow my unicycle, thinking it is without my knowledge, as
I know you have done, please take care to use gloves. Take care to
cooperate with the forces of eternal law. When you engage in wireless
communication, both within your home and without it, do so with care.
If you are outdoors, with something to say, take especial care when
you say it: project your voice, choose the appropriate words, and be
sure to enunciate.

THE LAPIDARY

He is in love with his words.

With the words he chooses and how he combines them and what the combinations mean to him and what he hopes they mean to others.

Lying awake late at night, he thinks about them, obsesses over them. He feels they hold great, mysterious truths about the world.

During the day, on street corners and park benches, he sells his words to mothers pushing strollers and lawyers on lunchbreaks and joggers in spandex.

When they pass by, he takes his words, rolls them around in his mouth, and spits them out as though they were precious pearls he could string together with his lips.

SKYSCAPES

They talk to you about the sky, about lifting them up to it, or your having fallen from it, as though these were things a person would want.

You are not averse to conversations about the sky. For example, you would want them to tell you about snowflakes, flying machines, the aurora borealis. You would enjoy time spent looking at cloud formations.

But they do not understand: they are not from where you are from; they think this is the way to have their way with you.

They try again. Now they tell you about who they have played against, what they have done best, how far they have gone.

They tell you about the palace they bought for the family they do not have. In the courtyard, the brown water in the pond of goldfish rises and falls mysteriously, until one day the fish are poisoned by paint chips they mistake for pellets.

They tell you about their church on an island of palm trees. When the tide is in and the waves are good, their god approves of surfing and cancels mass.

They tell you about the movie they filmed in a café that serves mint tea and Turkish delight. People move through the movie as through life: without props, special effects, or second takes.

You take these stories of lives lived in warmer and wilder climes and you twist them and you turn the tellers of them around. Now you do the telling.

You tell them about an airplane that flew you to a country house in the mountains. The driver, who was from the town your father was born in and spoke the language he thinks in, looped the plane once, twice, thrice, then landed it in a field of flowers.

You tell them about towers of gold. At sunrise, they are ochre, amber, rose, but when you stand beneath them, they are grey, the spaces filling silently with snow.

You tell them about will-o'-the-wisps and spectres steaming through winter forests and about night skies that are jade, aqua, that glow.

What they want to know, they begin to say. But they are turned around; it comes out wrong: as a plea, as laughter, as birdsong.

BIRD SUIT

You put on your bird suit. It's a little tight around the wings but you make do. You consult the manual. Take the front window, it says, and spread your wings. A tilt here, a lift there, you'll get the hang of it. You take flight. You soar through the cerulean life you thought you had forgotten. A life of nests, sturdy perches, eggs bearing offspring. Of trips down south. And perspective. There it is, still intact, not a cloud in it. Only thing is, it's no longer yours to live.

AIRBORNE

They agreed that together they were lightness. For days, the hours hidden from the sun and the neighbours would lift her up, lift him up. Their lightness could sift swiftly through them and it could travel: on airplanes from winter to summer and city to sea; on buses and subways from dusk to dark. When one of them had travelled some distance from the other, when they were in a warmer season or surroundings, or doing some other activity with some other person, they might suddenly discover they were airborne. They might remain aloft for hours or days, suspended in that hidden place, before finally they came back down.

THE CITY BELOW

It is true there are no dolphins or deep-sea divers, no sea mist or sailboats.

We cannot go for a swim when it is hot out and there is no sand to lie on, no sun to dry the drops of water and leave salty trails on our skin.

We cannot build castles with elaborate motes that fill until their walls collapse, and there are no seashells to collect, no pebbles to launch into the foam.

It is true that instead of waves on the shore we hear car horns and trains against tracks and elevator doors opening and closing, the elevator going up and down, to and from the twentieth floor.

But it is also true that when it takes us there and opens into the dark and damp hallway, we open the door to our apartment, and the city below us is the sea all around us.

It is true that there are no anemones or schools of fish, no pirate ships or sunken treasure.

But there are flower stands at midnight and barbecued meat at midday and green parrots in the palm trees.

People are eating in cafés and smoking on patios and walking their dogs. Some of them are walking other people's dogs.

And floating on the city is the uninterrupted sky, and we are prone to looking at it and opening a window onto it, and when the sun is setting, and instead of dark grey the city is golden, a breeze comes off it and we are content to do nothing more than watch it.

CITY LIVING

Our first impressions of city living are not so good. Many hours each day are spent below the ground or in dark tunnels: we take the metro, ride the elevator, try to avoid the frightening parkings. Even when we are outside our home, we are inside buses, buildings, cafés. We try to find the air-conditioned ones. The city's heat is tremendous and we pass potent garbage smells. We see many naked men lying on the street, even at night. They miss the exciting city nights, when other men and women dress in fashionable ropes. We do enjoy the rich gastronomy, cultural offerings, and live spectacles, even on a Monday. In the main plaza, a dancing water fountain displays special light effects. On the weekend, local people relax in Memory Park with their youngest ones. We go too. We visit the artificial lake and small ships. It is the biggest green space of the capital city. You can make several open-air activities like bicycling and rollers. Afterward, you can go for ice cream. Many say the most exquisite ice creams can be tasted in the city. We have found this to be true.

SUGAR DREAMS

At the grocery store I fill my shopping cart to overflowing: candy loops and bumble pie and cream whip and sweet milk. I ride down the hill from the parking lot to the playground. A good game of tic-tac-toe, followed by a toboggan run. I lie under a tree. The clouds are laced, just as I suspected. Out come the sugar dreams, each one sweeter than the next. Two dark clowns float over. Hello, they say. The short clown holds a deck of cards. He fans them and asks me to pick one. So many cards, so hard to choose. I do my best, but the clouds are disappointed. Their faces fall and it begins to rain. The rain is cold and the clowns clear out. Now the sky is blue again. So bright, I shield my eyes with the card I have chosen. On it, a bullfrog jumps through hoops of fire, each smaller than the last. This frog I recognize. We go way back, I say, but he doesn't know it. The flames are so close now that I start to burn up. I take off my socks and shoes, but nothing helps. Finally, when I can stand it no longer, the frog reaches the final hoop. He makes it through okay. Now, on the other side, I inspect myself. Singed by the flames, I am slightly black around the edges but in otherwise impeccable form.

SOME SHENANIGANS

It began with some shenanigans and continued from there. They were constructing themselves, after all: writing their story. It was the same old story, but brand new to them, wrapped as it was in silk or some other fine fabric. They did not even know where they were or when it was: the week before or the morning after. Entire days in funny hats and tree forts; silver suns and river runs. The days wove together—sienna days, olive days, cerulean days that wound from the ground up until one day they wound down. It was the end of friendship. No more witty banter and speech coinciding; too many conundrums and sleep disturbances. Entire days of intermittent showers, puffs of smoke, coffee grounds. So low down, they saw no ships on the horizon, no islands, no distant shore.

THE ISLAND

I spend two weeks on the island. My friends come to visit. A bosom friend, a flirtatious friend, and a friend I had forgotten. They bring rations: poultices and potions, short stories and logbooks, popsicles, playing cards. We set up camp.

My bosom friend reads to me. She describes greener and rockier islands to me. Tells of birds with feathers like mirrors that shimmer and shake. She smooths my sheets and warns of the flirtatious friend.

He arrives two days late, too early in the day. He lights a fire and removes the sheets from me. Braids my hair and runs off and finds a ladybug and lets it crawl on me. We share a popsicle. He drips onto me. We play cards. My friend loses one game, and another, and then he no longer wants to play. He prepares a poultice and a potion, and finishes it, forgetting to offer me any. Now he shimmers and shakes. He wants to explore, though he knows I can't come along. The next day, at dawn, he is gone. All morning, I look up at the sky. The island seems barren and dry. I send out a smoke signal.

Late at night, a voice comes calling. A friend from another time or place lies down next to me. He slips a ribbon from the pages of a logbook. Tells tall tales about distant ports of call. Talks of tigerfish and sea mist and palm oil. He brings news of inclement weather. The chimes and bells begin clinking. I've been thinking, my friend says, but the wind whisks his voice away. We wrap ourselves in the flapping sheets and follow the storm clouds across and then off the island.

RETURN FROM A LONG DREAM

I've returned from a long dream, the old father at the bus station said to me. We were riding our bikes east along the coast. When the sun was too hot and we were too tired to go on, we got off and crossed the sand to the ocean. There was no one else on the beach and we ran to the water and swam until the sun set it on fire. Afterward, we lay under the palm trees and fell asleep.

The old father rubbed his eyes and focused them on me. You're not Rosa, he said. Where's Rosa?

I looked around. The station was full of people. They were moving at different speeds and in different directions, but none of them were coming toward us.

I sat with the man for a while, waiting, though I knew Rosa wouldn't appear.

Finally, he got up and grabbed a worn backpack from the floor and walked over to a bike. It was a red road bike, in good condition, and clean, except for its tires, which were covered in sand.

REST ASSURED

You may find, on your return, that the apartment has been taken over by insects. Rest assured, with the exception of the giant moth that now lives in your bedroom, they will do you no harm. It is just a matter of getting used, for example, to the dense cloud of fruit flies in the kitchen, which will keep out of your way provided you flail your arms wildly before sitting down for a meal, or the trail of ants that has formed between the front door and the cookie jar. You'll have no problem stepping over it. Speaking of the cookie jar, you'll want to inspect all dry goods before consuming them. I have discovered larvae and mysterious cotton-like formations in the rice, kidney bean, and oatmeal jars. Although there are, of course, no fruits in the bathroom, there are flies. They seem drawn to the toilet water, so you might want to flush once or twice before sitting down on the bowl. You might also want to avoid the bidet, as a small family of brown scorpions now lives there. The shower remains in working order. In the evening, large numbers of armoured green bugs fly in through the windows I leave open to let in the cool air. By morning they've usually all died, forming piles under the windowsills. They can be swept up easily enough with the brooms I place in each room for that purpose. The mosquitoes are everywhere. Not much can be done about that. As to the moth, you'd do well to avoid using all artificial lighting, including the lamp on your night table, the fixture hanging from the ceiling, your computer, and your cellphone. You may also wish not to light candles or strike matches or smoke anything that requires a flame to burn. Due to the moth's size and erratic movements, it would be in your best interest to stick to these suggestions, at least for the time being.

IN THE COUNTRY

Welcome to the country. We hope you will feel at home among the great heights, lovely slopes, and significant textures. Our privileged region offers the best solar exposition all year round. In the spring, bold soils and deep colours are common because of the rain. During the summer, the air is full of unique perfumes. Though the heat can be spectacular in January and February, you can always wet yourself in the stream. In the harvest season, our strong aromas and exciting flavours will please you. Though the air is fresh, each day includes many hours of sunshine. This time of year, you will witness the excellent maturing of fruits and you can even select and eat some of them. We think winter is the preferred time to visit us here in the country: when the air is cold, we have very powerful sunsets.

BOIPEBA

After the sun sets, we leave the village for the houses along the shore.
The moon is full and the tide is in. We walk the plank. We climb higher
and higher above mudflats and flotsam. When we reach their house, two
storeys above the sea, the door is neither open nor closed. Outside it, on
a muddy mat: flip-flops and fruit peels. On the other side, which is not
exactly inside, their house: three walls, a roof, and four cement beams;
there was neither money nor materials to finish it. Their child sits on
the wood floor in a pink bikini. We say hello, and she blinks at us. Back
beyond bobbins and buckets and bins and nets are her parents, their
friends, our neighbours, watching the sea. The moon appears to be melting
into it. We lick our lips and taste salt. Water pours through the cement
beams below us. Want a drink? our neighbours say. They hand us
a beer and we sit down to watch the waves with them. A pink lizard
appears, flicking its tongue. For a while, no one says any old thing. Then
someone does. Tonight is thick as thieves, this person says, and we are
fairly sure we know what he means.

BEACH DAY

I'd like to do today what we did yesterday: leave behind the accoutrements
of sleep and our beds in the forest, pack sandwiches wrapped in
parchment paper, take the trail to the fourth beach, lie down in the sand
and drift into sleep as though to a distant island, wake up, dry off, think
less and then not at all about the persons from our pasts or uncertain
futures, roll over, unwrap our sandwiches, tell stories we've told before,
turn the pages of our sandy books, float into sleep and wake as though in
the waves, look up at the cloudless sky and out at the pine trees, dry off,
turn the sandy pages of our books, think carefully about where to watch
the sunset, settle in as the sky flushes at the thought, brush those persons
out of our minds again as the sky sighs loudly and then goes out.

WATERLOGGED

He lived for seven months at the bottom of my heart. He rented a cheap apartment there and spent weeks inside it, ordering takeout and watching TV. The smell of fried food and the constant chatter filled the rooms. Rain seeped under the door during heavy storms, the faucet leaked, and eventually the toilet clogged. Waterlogged, I was rotting from the inside out. I stopped eating. My friends tried to help. They brought soup and muffins and sang to me. One of them slow-danced with me. But it was no use. Beyond my window, up above, and down below, the days flowed slowly by. Grey days of storm clouds and winter coats. Then longer days, sharper days, until one day, there he stood, outside my window. Tattered and torn. Overgrown and overweight. I did not wave hello. Beyond the glass, in the street, he looked up at me, then down on me. I remembered the way he could look. I closed the curtains. A few days later I saw him again, in the rain, without an umbrella, surrounded by soggy cardboard, bubble wrap, and duffel bags. He placed each of these items, which contained all his items, in a van, then he got in the van with a woman I didn't know he knew, and she drove it away.

I RUN INTO D

Hello, I say.

Hello, he says.

There is a test: it is warm again, between us.

The temperature is right for more words. It appears we don't know any.

But then: I'm glad to see you've put on weight, he says.

And then: I'm glad to see you're balding, I say, though he isn't, though he won't be the next time I see him, when I'll wish I had commented instead on the wrinkles around his eyes, or the sagging pouches of skin below them, or on his posture, which was always poor and is now much worse, or better yet, on his new girlfriend, who by then will be his old girlfriend.

I'll wish I had commented on her, on the violent lipstick on her teeth, on her suede boots and bright rain jacket, her long, bleached hair and painted nails, and how all these colours and textures did not look very good together, on her, and beside him.

OLD FATHERS

Most of them are old fathers. Rarely, a young father appears. You can tell because his wings, which are bright blue, have not yet been clipped. He is free to fly in and around the jail, and he may choose a young mother or an old one. Most prefer old mothers. We suspect this is because of their life experience; old mothers have been around the block, so to speak. Once he makes his choice, the mating takes place, and he becomes an old father. We clip his wings, and he is no longer free to come and go as he pleases.

PEOPLE START TO BE BORN

It begins with your ex-boyfriend. You do not mean that he has been born again. He has not found a leader, religious or otherwise; he has not changed his career or purchased a fast car. This man has had a son, then a daughter. Then other people have daughters. People who know people you know, and then people you know yourself: your greengrocer, your kinesiotherapist, and the woman who hired you, then fired you. They name their daughters after birds and blackberries, dew and dawn, happiness and solitude. You get to know these daughters, through pictures sent to you on your phone. They wear giraffes, crescent moons, red cabooses.

When these daughters are older, and you are over, you read books to them. They pick books about seafarers, farm animals, and flying insects. Together, you give serious consideration to the trials and tribulations of these creatures. You study the way they are rendered. You agree they are funny-looking. Their heads are too big, their colours all wrong.

One daughter would like to draw her own. Daughter on lap at the kitchen table, you draw the sky. In it, she draws giant red-and-blue bumblebees, a butterfly with turquoise heart-shaped wings, and some very hairy caterpillars. She colours the sky—the parts of it where the insects are not—indigo. This sky has not a single cloud in it.

This daughter's sister wants to paint a farm. You paint her a big one. It has plenty of land for animals to graze on and a red barn. She draws purple piglets with green snouts and a horse with stripes like a zebra. She plants crops: corn on the cob, mushrooms, watermelon trees. The watermelons she colours bright blue.

Another daughter decides to draw an ocean. In it, seafarers frolic with octopuses. A sea anemone eats a banana. The moon, which is the colour of pink frosting, is full over this ocean, and once the daughter has drawn it and carefully filled it, her eyes begin to close, and she sways to sleep as though she were afloat in it.

FRANKLIN HAS A TREMENDOUS WILL TO LIVE

Franklin is sixteen years old and he is a senior citizen. Because he has kidney failure, Franklin is often hungry and he always has to pee. Black goo gets stuck to his face but he is too tired to clean it. He sleeps. He does not groom. He rarely goes outdoors to enjoy the garden and fresh air, and he no longer chases butterflies and chickadees.

Not long ago, Franklin lost his life partner, Lionel. They had been together for many years and though they sometimes fought, sometimes viciously, their lives were lived in each other's.

After Lionel was gone, Franklin was quieter, and then he was slower. He began to move less and now he hardly moves at all. In the winter, his cushion is placed next to the heat vent and he is welcome to spend the day on top of it, sleeping and occasionally licking his private parts, now that Lionel's are no longer available. In the summer, the window is left open so he might benefit from the breeze without having to leave the comfort of his cushion. During the day, he is served plenty of tuna fish, and every evening, before bed, salmon-flavoured treats are delivered to his side. He eats them all and meows until he is allotted a second portion. He devours this portion, too, and then throws up the undigested pellets. Orange stains on beige carpet radiate from the cushion, becoming less frequent and finally disappearing altogether at the limits of the living room, for Franklin is no longer able to climb the stairs to the top floor nor descend them to the basement, where his litter box was once located. Now it is located next to his cushion.

HOMESICK

He lived for seven years at the bottom of my heart. He built a beautiful house there. It had high ceilings and was full of natural light and healthy plants that hung down from the shelves and rafters. He also had a fat tomcat. The two of them spent a lot of time indoors. They walked to and fro and clearly didn't get much sleep. I couldn't sleep either. I shuffled around in bed, listening to them shuffle around the house. It was awful when they had guests over, worse still when they had one guest and it was a woman. I didn't want to know what was going on in his life, but they talked loudly and of course I heard them. Sometimes, however, he lowered his voice to a whisper and I knew then that he was talking about me, though I was never able to make out what he was saying. The cat didn't bother me much but I wanted him to leave. I wanted him to go out for groceries every now and then or to go for a stroll or, better yet, on vacation.

Years passed, and I began to think he'd never leave. But when I least expected it, first for fleeting moments, then for longer ones, I didn't hear him. I might be chatting with a friend for a while and forget him. But afterwards, there he was; he'd always return. Other times I might be involved in some activity—I wrote awful, impassioned poetry then, and swam laps at the community centre—and everything was quiet inside. I couldn't tell you when it happened exactly, but more years passed, and without realizing it, I found that I didn't think of him very often, and then not at all.

GOOD RIDDANCE

Take the front window and the footpath. Follow the goldenrods and foxgloves down to the bridge. Cross the river. Look for the raft with your name on it. Hop on and drift to another place. Arrive at that place sometime later. Climb into it, through the shadows. Find the shadow that looks like the person you thought you had forgotten. You may wish to nod hello. Follow this person through the ghost forest. Keep going until you reach the wild blackberries. Have your fill. Just beyond them you will see a wood cabin. Climb into it, through the window. The bed will be made up with fresh sheets. For some days, sleep in it; sleep in, in it. Arrange the pillows and dream in it. When you dream the front door is unlocked, get out of bed and open it. You will find a dirt road in front of it and a motorbike driving past. Hop on and hitch a ride. Ride for many hours or days until you reach the smokestacks and factories at the edge of the city. Circumvent the city. Opt instead for the country. Drive through cornfields and bales of hay. Climb one hill, and then all the hills, and then climb off and take in the view. You may find that you are taken back by the view. Back many years by the farms and fields, the currents of air, and the roads in rows that lift, to that voice, its lilt. Follow the voice up and over to the place you last were, when last you heard it. Lie down and stretch out in that place. Take sweet sleep in that place. When you dream of the words you thought you had forgotten, wake to find them on the tip of your tongue. Spit one word out after another. Good riddance to bad words. Now, wipe your eyes, stretch your legs, and wash your hands of that place.

FLOODWATER

We pulled up to the banks of our house. We clambered out of the canoe
and ate the ham sandwiches Father had brought. Pigs had been snuffing
about for truffles, and the smell of life on the verge of death did not please
us. We got back in and paddled through the door, past our refrigerator,
which was floating. It was leaking a liquid of indeterminate colour. The
TV also floated past and I mourned that loss loudly. Good riddance, said
Father, but Mother and Brother were also making sorrowful noises. That
disappointment weighed a lot, but it did not sink us. The stairs were
underwater and bubbles rose to the surface. Did this mean life there down
below? Brother wondered. We rowed over to the master bedroom. We got
a good look at it all from up there. The jackdaws were very active. They
flew in strange formations. Look, a horse, said Brother. For a second,
the birds did seem to be galloping. The sun started to set over our town,
the schoolhouse, the police station, the pub, Jemma and Phil's across the
street, the O'Connors' down the lane. All these townspeople's homes and
buildings had filled with water too. Only they weren't out paddling in it.
They had in fact drowned in it.

SOMETIMES YOU HEAR HORSES

You don't know if they are crossing the mountains in your mind or the cobblestones of the street below your bedroom. You linger on the threshold between sleep and wakefulness. The sun comes in slowly with the songs and sirens of the city. The horses are out there, you think, and you hear their hooves, the car horns, the motorbikes. Your eyes are open now; now, they close. You roll onto your stomach, stretch your limbs out to the cool corners of the bed. You lie there listening to the city wake against the heat. The morning is heavy and still, and it pushes you back into the mountains, where a cold wind blows. The horses are louder in the rarefied air; you hear them gallop under you, and all around you. They take you up into the clouds, and rain begins to fall. You shiver, but when you wake, the sheets are damp and twisted beneath you, the heat of the city wrapped around you.

DUERMEVELA

Can't we just bob and list and watch the dream
clouds sift through the city? But you get up, and
you let yourself out, and you drift into the heat
of it.

EL TAXISTA

I was a hot horse, he said. He did not look like a horse;
he did not look like he could gallop.

I was a hot, hot horse in the mountains, he said.
But he was in Buenos Aires now, driving a taxi
late one night.

For ten years, I did not leave the mountains.
Now I don't hardly leave the city, he told me.

In the city, it had not finished raining.

He drove fast, past the other cars on the road,
his face flushed, flashing ruby, emerald, gold.

Where do you come from and where are you going?
he wanted to know.

The moon, I said: I was in no mood for chitchat.

Sure thing, he said, and started to accelerate.
Soon, we were racing through the liquid night.

Beyond the wet windows: sky rises and neon lights,
bus shelters, pizza parlours. Then the dark river,
the weeping willows. The horizon.

The taxi began to climb. It climbed and wound around
and then down and then all the way up into the mountains.

Outside, the damp dark had become white; the rain, snow.
I could see my breath but said nothing. I rubbed my hands
together.

Thick snowflakes slid down the windows.
Suddenly, beyond them, three horses, white and wild,
galloping alongside us.

Caballos cimarrones, he said, and in the snowy dawn,
he lowered one window, then another,
and slowed the car to a stop.

GOLDFISH

It has been raining for years, though only under the city's trees, so people avoid the jacarandas and eucalyptus and take shelter beneath the open sky instead. Pools of water have collected under the trees' branches, and bacteria and small orange fish live in them. The fish swim to and fro and in circles around the trunks. They reproduce, and more small orange fish are born. Soon the pools' surfaces become dimpled with their gaping mouths; they have eaten all the bacteria and there is no more food in the water. Some of the fish try to flip-flop to another pool in search of food, though most die, and the pools turn orange but not gold.

THE POND

Most of them are old fathers. At the park, that is.

They sit on benches in front of the jungle gym or next to the pond. Their hair, if any remains, is grey or snow white, and their spines are curved.

The young fathers are the ones playing on the jungle gym or swimming in the pond.

The former takes place in the springtime or the fall, and the latter in the summer months, which are stifling.

You can hardly keep the young fathers out of the pond in the summer, even though it is coated with a layer of brown slime, and empty beer cans and bags of chips float on the surface.

Large goldfish, which are actually orange, lurk in the water's depths and swim between and around the legs of the young fathers.

When the young fathers finally emerge from the pond, they too are coated with brown slime.

This disgusts their children, who know better than to swim in the pond, and who prefer old fathers.

MEMORY PARK

Not well, can you help? said the old father on the park bench as I walked by.

He wore a helmet and cycling pants. He was in very good physical condition.

Next to him, a red bike leaned against the bench. It was an expensive bike and bags were packed neatly in front of the handlebars and tucked behind and beside the seat.

On the ground in front of the old father was a wool hat with a few coins in it. I placed one coin in the hat. It clinked against the others and he looked straight at me.

You look just like her, he said. Though she would be much older than you now.

Like who? I asked.

Rosa, he said. You haven't seen her, have you?

I shook my head. Where could she be? I asked.

She's gone, he said. We were travelling together. All the way up from the south and then east along the shore. For two years we travelled together, then one day we were on the beach, and when I woke, she was gone.

By now, the sun was beginning to set and Memory Park was cold and angry.

We were not near the beach.

Why don't you go back there? I said anyway. Maybe you'll find her. Maybe someone has seen her.

She's gone, he said, much louder this time, and I jumped and walked quickly away.

SEQUINS AND PAINTED SKIN

Boys, I have brand-new makeup on, she said, though no one was around to hear her.

She said it louder, and then she screamed it, and all the pigeons lifted up and flew west, then east, then settled down on the other side of Memory Park.

She settled down too and began to sing. She sang sweetly and the pigeons flew up again and joined her.

Some of them cooed.

Not long after, she painted her pointed lips to the sky and it turned an electric pink. The city's water-stained buildings, rusted balconies, and palm trees slowly lost their colours for the day.

She dusted her eyes midnight blue, and out of the shadows people moved into the plaza.

Soon it was full of them and the cool night air. They sat down on the stone benches and lay about in the patches of grass. She heard their words and sighs, their silences.

Brand-new makeup on! she said, as a boy walked by. He was not wearing a shirt.

Hello, beautiful, she whispered.

The boy walked quickly until he was past her. He had tried not to look, but there she was, sequins and painted skin, a swivel chair, high heels, a smile that confused him.

CLEANLINESS

Girls, I am clean now, he said, and though parts of him were hidden from us, he did emit a glow.

Very good, we said, and moved closer, then closer still, to inspect him.

We began with his head: few hairs were left on it, and he made soft little sounds as we parted them this way and that.

He sighed, then was silent when we looked in his ears and up as far as we could into his mouth and nose.

Then down we went, inch by inch, and he squirmed while we searched in his creases and folds.

Onward, we said, to your fingers and toes, and he began to giggle in spite of himself, then inside of himself, and soon he was writhing from pain or from laughter.

We laughed, too, until we saw what we were looking for, and in an instant, all was still.

Where to next? he said, after a long pause, as though he didn't know exactly where he was going.

DENTAL HYGIENE

Every morning, the men would pick up long wooden brushes, and they would clean thoroughly, from top to bottom. They would remove bits of food, plant matter, day-old decay. They would sweep this debris from under the gums and trees until the city's teeth were gleaming.

TOOTHBRUSHES AND SPONGES

Toothbrushes and sponges for sale, said the old father on the street corner as the businesswomen and men walked by.

He had laid out his goods, organized by colour, on a stained bedsheet.

One sponge please, I said.

What colour? he asked. There were five to choose from.

Blue, I said.

He looked carefully at the sponges and handed me a yellow one. Anything else? he asked.

Next to the sheet, in a small tin box, he had placed other items: rusted keys around a ring, seashells, a bottle of sunscreen with a peeling label, and three yellowing photos.

How much for the sunscreen? I asked.

It's not for sale, he said.

What about the seashells?

No, he said, and you can't have the keys either.

He handed me the pictures then. I told him I didn't want his old photographs.

Please take them, he said, and began to cry.

I shook my head.

Take them, he shouted, and I did, and walked away.

When I reached the next block, I looked at the photographs. Two were of an old red bicycle with no rider. The third was badly damaged, though I could make out the shape of a woman's face and, behind it, the sea.

PHOTOGRAPHS

The only pictures he ever wanted to take of you were pictures in which
you were naked. You did not say yes at first, and he did not take your
picture. He did not take your picture when, finally, you travelled together
to the island he had shown you on a map when you met, and you stood
looking at the sea, while you felt him look up you, then down; not when
you went out for Peruvian food, for one last dinner, and you were golden,
opposite each other, and you took his picture, before you went away; nor
when you returned, bronzed and blue, after months in the sun. By then
you had many pictures of him. Most of them he had taken of himself
and sent to you: him getting on or off the motorbike he had ridden over
the Andes, getting in or out of the shower, getting high with friends. It
is not untrue that you looked at these pictures often. You looked at him,
at all the angles and shades of him, and you did not wonder, at first, why
he was not interested in looking at a digital and dressed version of you.
Certainly, he was interested in being looked at, and you obliged him;
you even showed his pictures to your friends. It is not untrue that he is
good-looking, you said, and they rolled their eyes and said nothing. When
they did say something was when you began to talk more of him, at times
only of him, which was when you felt the first of the carefully calculated
indifferences he wedged between you. But it was only when he began to
send fewer pictures, and then no pictures, until, finally, he did send one,
and you were not sure if it was an accident, this picture of another woman,
standing naked in his living room, that you began to wonder wildly about
his pictures, and about yours.

MY FRENCH IS RUSTED

Like a nail, holding together an old picture frame. The picture it frames shows me, when I was a young child. I am one child, of four, in the picture. The four of us play in the mud. There is mud on one child, then on another. Soon, all the children are covered in mud. The mud is dark, the children light, against the sky. In the sky there is a small plane. Behind the plane, a message: Où est Pierre? One of us is called Pierre. He is me. I am looking up, and out, at the sky. In the sky there is now a small cloud, then it is a big cloud, then a grey cloud. From the cloud falls a fat drop of rain. The sky claps, then turns black. From the black comes all the rain. It washes away the mud, rusts the nail, stains the picture frame.

I'LL BRING THE CLOUDS

Is what she said. He wondered how she would do it and how soon.

I'll let you know, she said, but it was cold outside and she was tired and had to walk the dog and water the plant, which was dying, was possibly already dead.

The next morning she had to wake up early for work, and while she was at work, there were many small things she had to do so that other, bigger things could be done by other, bigger people.

When she was done work, she'd been meaning to start exercising, and the floor had to be swept and the laundry done, and she wanted to finish the book she was reading.

The book was on happiness, on where to find it, and how to know when you had. She was having a tough time getting through it, getting through everything, really, so she told him that next Friday might work, or the Friday after, though she never did end up finding the time.

A DOG NAMED FACUNDO

This letter is to certify that Ms. Stella Maris Echevarria, who has been my patient for three years, and whose life story I am totally acquainted with, including her unnatural and errant son, Arturo, a man of treacly words and weak actions, her circulation problems, both municipal and sanguinary, the bell that does not cease to toll in her left ear, her voice, in which day is eternally sinking into night, her aversion to intermittent echoes, perfumed persons, and asymmetrical spaces, and her left foot, which is larger than the right and cannot be housed adequately in footwear. She tends to her garden, she tells me, but there is evidence of wilting and decay. Considering these functional and other limitations, she has been prescribed an emotional support pet, and it is important that they travel together, both internally and externally, as he has been shown to alleviate her symptoms.

PEOPLE WHO TOUCH INSTRUMENTS

Some people who touch instruments at first do so by accident. What they really want is to touch someone, or to be touched by someone.

But in the absence of anyone, in the absence even of a pet such as a cat or a hamster, they turn to a musical instrument.

The first touch is, of course, tentative. They are not sure where to place their left hand or their right. They are not sure if their touch is too soft or too forceful. They don't want to hurt the instrument.

Soon, they learn what to do and the instrument responds: it makes a sound. Not a human sound like a sigh or that of a domesticated animal, but one made in response to the person's touch.

This is pleasurable and they would like to make another.

They touch the instrument in more or less the same way and it makes a second sound more or less like the first. They move their hands faster, then slower, then faster again.

They are letting loose.

The sounds they make are not pleasant exactly, but they go on making them since they start to feel pretty good, and then pretty great.

NOT WHAT YOU SHOULD BE DOING

I like Kenny G's music because it helps me to cry.

If months or even years have passed since I last shed a tear, if nothing seems to help, then I turn on the FM radio.

I look for a station that plays adult contemporary music and wait for the sounds of Kenny G; I find that the wail of his saxophone works best.

At first I listen quietly: we are just getting reacquainted and I'm still feeling a bit shy. But then Kenny G warms up and I start to feel loose too.

Soon I can tell there's something he wants to ask me, though he's not sure how to say it. I wait and listen a little longer, and finally, just as the synthesizer kicks in, Kenny G can contain himself no longer.

"What are you doing with your life?" he wants to know.

I don't have a good answer, or any answer really.

But Kenny G does. "Not what you should be doing," he says. "Not at all what you should be doing."

SHOULDS

Hair should be cut, pimples popped, lines in neck straightened out.
Posture should be adjusted. Should stop biting fingernails. Starting with
pinky fingernails. Should exercise again, and meditate: one session in
the morning, one in the evening, of meditation, possibly also of exercise.
Should get eight or ideally nine hours of sleep. Should get these hours
every night, but especially on weeknights. Racing thoughts, repetitive
thoughts, and the occasional raunchy thought should be ignored. More
essential fatty acids should be consumed as part of diet. More heme
iron. Fewer sugars, including fruit sugars. No more ice cream. Should
eat until less full, no filling up until too full. Should organize life. Inner
life and outer life. Starting with undergarments. Then proceeding to
outergarments. Not neglecting adornments. Should find life partner,
if not for life then for immediate future. Or not-so-distant future.
Should devise plan for future. A good, solid plan for future. For more
money in the future. Also should see about more money in the present.
Two or preferably three times more money in the present. Should give
more presents, to friends and family, not necessarily friends of family.
Should send emails, long emails or short. And instant messages. To say
hello. Twice or thrice a week. When it is convenient, not when work
should be done. Should work more efficiently. Full days of efficiency, on
paid work. Should avoid poorly paid work. Also work that doesn't pay.
Should play. Out of doors. In the woods. Should climb more trees. Swim
with frequency in the sea. If possible, the Mediterranean Sea. Or else the
Caribbean Sea. Just as long as it is a turquoise sea.

AT THE SEASHORE

Welcome to the seashore. It is hot here, but the wind blows fresh. Why
not go down to the calm waters, which are ideal for relax. The beach is
not too crowded and it is easy to find an isolated and marvellous site of
sand. The only conversation you will have there is with yourself, unless
you are with your family. Then the youngest ones can make miniature
castles while you read a news magazine or bestselling book. The beach is
populated with public toilets, first aid rooms, and parkings. If you want
to get physical, there are many nautical activities to enjoy, for example
scuba diving and snorkelling. The area has very wealthy sea life. There
are lapwing birds, piebald dolphins, and sea wolves. Until May, there
are pinguinos. The biggest continental colony in the world is south
of here, with over a million exemplars. Along the coastal promenade,
fishermen show their passion for the sport. You can eat what they capture
in beachside shacks that have a fine sea cuisine. Many accommodations
are available at the seashore. There are oversize hotels, campings, and air
breakfasts where you can lie in a hammock and listen to the singing birds.
Some amazing excursions are found nearby. Don't forget to visit the ruins
from the Second World Wide War, and during the summer, to stop at the
market, where local artisans are for sale.

BELOW THE WAVES

Help, please help! the goat cries. The passersby do nothing. It is hot out and they are going to the seashore.

The goat's ankles are tied. He is being carried by a man.

In the man's other hand is a suitcase. Next to him is a large woman wearing loud lipstick and a sundress.

Help, please help! the goat cries again. His tears fall into the ocean.

Shut up! the man says, but the goat doesn't listen.

Upside down, bound, the goat is frightened. He watches the wooden slats of the boardwalk and the violent sea below it. Rainbow-coloured fish swim up to the surface and the woman and man stop to watch them in the waves.

Then the goat squirms and the man sweats and the goat slips from his hand. He drops into the ocean. The suitcase drops in next to him.

Below the waves, the sea is no longer violent. The fish swim to the goat and suitcase, surround them, and swim silently down with them. They land softly in a hollow in the coral.

The suitcase breaks open. In it are things the woman and man need on their vacation: a bikini and swimming trunks, beach towels, a transistor radio, a package of prophylactics. The package of prophylactics breaks open and rainbow-coloured condoms drift out and settle into the sand.

The fish inspect them, the goat settles in next to them, and the radio begins to play. It plays Tom Zé and the goat sways far below the waves.

HYDROLOGY

They were a young couple and they had seemed so affable, so open to the world at first. It had been undeniably good: each was brand new to the other; one discovery rushed another. She had felt, during those first, fervent days of spring, that parts of them were flowing into her, that there was more of her than ever before. The feeling wouldn't last, of course, though it slipped away so subtly—not even unpleasantly—that at first she dismissed it. It must all be in my head, she told herself, and tried hard to believe it. But during the cumbersome days of summer, a new feeling took hold, an unrelenting pressure, and she began to sense that she was seeping out of herself. Soon, there was clearly less of her; parts of her that had once been easy to find seemed lost for good. Finally, unable to take it any longer, she talked to them, which meant to him. He did not deny it. He understood, he said; he would talk to her about it. And he did, and for a time they eased up on her, and she felt more fully—more firmly—herself than ever before. And it didn't last. Again she felt their pressure, felt them squeeze entire parts of her out of her, and this time she resolved to talk directly to her about it. In a way, we're in the same position, she thought, there should be empathy here, from me to her and her to me. And so she talked to him about it, about talking to her about it, because he was always in the goddamn middle of it, and she'd been willing, he said, but there was confusion about where and when, and then no, she didn't seem willing any longer, and finally, he was the one to tell her, and what he told her was that there was nothing they could do, cared to do, and on hearing these words she felt they had wrung every last drop out of her and now there was none of her left.

WHAT DID YOU MEAN BY FLEETING?

The word is sopping wet. One by one, I wring out each of its meanings. I collect them in a blue bucket. For some time, they slosh around in there, each the answer to a question that rises and falls like the tide. Then I start to drown in answers. I want just one, the right one, but when I reach for it, it slips away. They all slip away. Stripped of meaning, the word no longer takes me to you, or away from you, or anywhere at all.

YOUR VOICE

They would like to borrow it. They would like to
use it to say words in your first language, which
is their second language, or not their language at
all. They marvel at the way you say words in this
language. Any old word will do: ocean, possum,
fleeting. It's hard for them to say these words.
They can't coordinate their tongues with their
teeth and lips. The words they say are similar,
but there is some fundamental difference,
some sound that comes out not as they would
like. They find this embarrassing when they
are sober. When they are not sober, and only
somewhat embarrassed by the sounds they
make, they no longer wish to borrow your voice,
or to hear it at all.

MAGNIFYING GLASS

Part of her face is paralyzed. It's the part around her eyes. The skin sags, which makes her look sad even when she is happy, or angry, or anxious. She can move only her mouth, so she has to use it and the shapes and sounds she makes with it, so people know how she feels. As a child she struggled with this, her laughter sometimes mistaken for tears. People often asked what was the matter when she was really having a very good time. But as she grew older, her voice became a precise instrument, and now it is what she is known for. Like a magnifying glass, it takes what cannot be seen by the naked eye and sharpens it, so that it can.

LOOK WHO IS TALKING

This is how to speak with your eyes. Face your interlocutor and lock into their gaze. Cock your head. Open your mouth but emit no sounds: no hiccups, whispers, sighs. Size them up. You might wish to convey warmth or hostility, altruism or egoism. You might want to share good times, or bad ones. You might like to take flight, and head south, or to the pond, in unison. You have tools for these communications. You have your eyelashes, your eyelids, your eyeballs. You might move these at different speeds or in different directions. You might avert your gaze—to the left or the right; up or down—and then return it to your interlocutor. Practice makes perfect.

Why speak with your eyes when you have lips, teeth, a tongue? When you have vocal cords? And you can use them to make words. Words on their own or in the company of others are not so good at saying thoughts and feelings: they might say one thing when you want to say another, the opposite thing, even; they might be ambiguous and mean several conflicting things, when you want to say just one; they might hint at something you'd rather keep hidden. The eyes do not deceive in this way, even if they do in others.

NO DANGER OF AN IMMINENT NATURE

The house looked abandoned. Mother was fearful but there seemed
no danger of an imminent nature. We had been out hunting in the
delta when we found it. All around us were shades of emptiness.
We had moved mesmerized through them. We had rowed until
we were knee-deep in them. Then we had pulled up next to the
house. It was on stilts over pacific waters. A frayed rope floated
beneath it. And a tangle of fishing wire. We sensed life nearby, but
it smelled like death. You first, said Mother, dropping anchor. I
did not mind; I climbed the soggy steps two at a time. The house
sighed loudly. Mother sputtered; she did not take this to be a good
omen. Don't fret, I said. The words did not work. Still, I went inside.
The house was rotten but well proportioned. There was shattered
glass and a splattering of an unknown nature; a gas stove but no
canister, a fridge but no food. There were mouldy clothes in a corner.
And plenty of buzzards. Skedaddle, I said to them; they ruffled their
feathers but did not go far. I went into the other room. I saw a rusted
bed frame, a soiled mattress, a mirror. In the mirror, the cracked
sky was a menace to the day. Light had largely disappeared from it.
Tormented clouds had gathered in it. The finest of rains began to
fall. I heard Mother splashing about down below. I went up to the
window. Everything all right? I said, but the voice that answered
belonged to another, and I saw Mother flailing and floundering, as
the day sunk into night.

MOTHERS AND DAUGHTERS

I think that was the first experience losing something from my heart.
I cried a lot when it was gone, mostly in bed, though sometimes I cried
on the bus, looking out the window while people looked at me, or just
walking down the street. I also had trouble with my appetite, which
disappeared. My face started to change: my cheeks withdrew and the skin
below my eyes became sallow. Creases formed on my forehead, and my
hair, which had been jet black, lost its shine and turned grey. I looked
older, or old, though only a year had passed, though I was pregnant again.

BIRTHDAY DINNER

A man walks past. His face is moulded like plasticine: substances have
been injected into it, his age removed from it. We sit down to dinner.
We order spreads of eggs and olives, cheeses, salamis. We open bottles
of wine. Children the age of men sell pens, socks, herbs from a cardboard
box. They offer discounts for Women's Day, for ageless beauty. A woman
the age of a child, holding a child, looks at the small plates, the glasses,
the scrunched and stained napkins, at what is left of what she does not
have, and we look not at the pits, the shells, the crusts, at what remains of
what we did, or at her—we do not look, really—and she moves on to the
next table.

BALVANERA

From a rectangle cut out of the sky in Balvanera falls food instead of rain. Lemon rinds, clementines, all day long. The sky turns yellow and orange. The air smells like freshly squeezed juice. Afterwards, the fruit covers the ground. It begins to rot, and a sickly sweet smell arises from the sticky pulp. Then eggshells, chicken bones, the left-over fat from some steaks drop down from above. The shells crack into tiny pieces and the fat absorbs the falling bones. Eventually, the worms and slugs find homes in the other animals. Lit cigarettes also fall from the sky. The embers blink, then go out. The paper slowly disintegrates, but the filters never break apart; they take on the brown colour of the soil and pile up in small mounds that eventually become big mounds.

THE FIRST CITY

That's when I started running, though not in circles. I did not always run in circles. At first, I ran forward; I was sure of it. I ran past palm trees and parakeets, fruit rotting on street corners, old men smoking in the heat, children playing hide-and-seek. I ran past exhaust fumes and car horns, red lights and traffic jams, past barbecue stands, moving vans. I ran right out of the city, I thought, and into the next one. The next city was nothing like the first, at first: the streets were wider and emptier; the traffic was quieter and the birds louder; the men taller, the women leaner; the city greener. There were bigger and brighter flowers in the trees. And perfumed trees, trees with fat purple leaves, and veiled trees with crowns I was sure I had never seen before. I ran past greengrocers and ice cream parlours. I stopped for ice cream. I had never been to this ice cream parlour; I did not know the man behind the counter who was sure he knew me. I ran from this man, and he ran after me, shaking his fist. I ran away over cobblestones and gnarled roots, under fig trees and lemon trees, until there were fewer trees, just a few spindly trees, ailing in ways I thought I had never seen before. I ran toward the brown river, for many kilometres I followed the stench of that river, over mud-filled puddles and plastic bottles and condom wrappers. I ran until the wind began to beat and the birds shrieked. The sky had turned pink, the river black. I entered a long, dark tunnel. Am I not running back, I thought, as this city, its fights and flights, its mess and men, its children, were beginning to look like the first.

RED RUBIES

There are rats down there, be careful, I say to the sparrow, but he does not seem to mind: he has found an orange fruit.

While the rats brood below, he tries to open it, which takes some time. Inside, there are red rubies.

Sweet, the sparrow sings, and plucks one from the creamy chest. He squishes it in his mouth and red juice drips onto the leaves.

He hums a tune. Another sparrow joins him, tries a ruby. More juice drips down and the rats look up. They see red, smell sugar.

Forget those rubies, I say, but the sparrows are busy singing. The rats are no singers, they are climbers, and there are riches among the leaves. The rats go straight for them.

Look out, they've taken the shortcut, I say, and for a moment the garden is silent and still. Then there is a gust of wind, and the fronds and leaves rattle and the sun's shapes shift.

One sparrow ruffles his feathers, looks at the rubies, flies high above the garden.

The other sparrow moves for the chest, gets a ruby, hums a tune.

A rat gets there next, gets a ruby. It's inside the sparrow.

More rats look up, see red, smell blood.

A RUN OF GOOD LUCK

I've had a run of good luck, the old father at the next urinal said to me. First an ice cream cone, then a ride on the Ferris wheel, then I found the beach.

We were in a worn and dusty town along the coast. It was no longer summer.

Which beach? I asked the man.

Her beach, he said. You see, I've finally found it.

How can you be sure? I asked.

She was down there in the sand with her friends, he said, and pointed toward the sea. All those years. She stayed behind. I couldn't have known it at the time, I was out of my mind.

And now? I asked.

I'm well, thanks, and yourself?

But before I could answer, he motioned for me to follow him. She's out there waiting, he said. Come meet her.

He led me out of the bathroom, but except for the two men still smoking in the corner, the bar was empty.

Without saying a word, he walked to the door. A red bike was parked in front of it and he got on, struggled to find his balance, and rode away.

ROCK YOUR BOAT

Lately, I have been thinking of you. What I have been thinking is that I saw you, in this city that is neither of our own. You were not on your own. I was concerned. Principally for myself. Also confused. About if I should write you. I did not want to rock you, to rock your boat. My intentions were far away from that. I remember when I would call on you. It was not always at the most opportune of times. Still, you let me in. And then out. On your balcony we would eat persimmons and listen to your neighbours fight. We were good listeners. Not such good talkers. I remember when you came right up to me in the middle of all those paintings and people. It is true that I did not at first let you in. And so you walked out. But you came back and we rode our bikes through the heat and the deserted streets to your apartment. You did not invite me in. And then out. When I saw you, so many years from home, I only wanted to see if you were well. I did not want to churn you, to churn your waters.

A ROYAL BLUE LIFE

What she had wanted most, all those years ago, was a royal blue life. She thought that now she might have one. She had thought, back then, that if one day her life took on this particular colour, she would want him to know; that his knowing this thing about her would be what really mattered. But it didn't matter. Not just because they no longer knew each other, no longer even had news of each other. He had long lost his way with her. Even so, she had to admit that she sometimes wondered if he could still have his way with others. Maybe he could. But she thought not. She thought it would probably be less easy for him to colour the lives of others as he had hers, though this would not be for lack of effort on his part.

GIFT ITEMS

D gave M, whom he saw once a week, his long johns—
though they were several sizes too big and smelled funny,
like something living had just died—and his earphones,
which were fully functional, and a contraption for
counting livestock, which served no obvious function.
D also gifted her numerous photos of himself in various
states of undress. He told her about a Cuban poet, his
favourite, and sent her a picture of a poem by this poet,
though he refused to loan her his books, which he was
never seen to be reading. M offered to loan D several
books, and he seemed interested in these books, but he
never remembered to take them when he walked out the
door. She gave D Mexican chili powder, which may have
been too spicy, and a plant with thick leaves, which may
have been diseased.

Before she was able to stop seeing D, M began to see
O, who gave her seeds that would ostensibly grow into
barley, beetroot, and cabbage, though she never planted
them, and fruit he picked in the river delta—blackberries,
tangerines, and lemons, which she froze, peeled, and
squeezed. She brought him sweets from the subtropics:
carob cubes, coconut candies, and sugary squares of
bananas. He carved her a pipe and filled it. She loaned
him a book and hid a note in it.

Prior to M, O had been with C, who had interviewed him for an article she never ended up writing, recommended music she never ended up sending, promised to prepare a meal she never ended up cooking. O spent a long time fitting blackout curtains to a large window in C's east-facing apartment, and he fixed C's cupboards and inspected her coffee machine, which had begun to produce weak coffee.

Most of the time, D lived and fought with J. On a trip overseas, not with J, but with M, D stopped by the dollar store and got J rainbow-coloured spatulas, dish towels with autumn leaves on them, a keychain made of a material that was pleasant to touch and shaped like a bear, pink leg warmers, and a knife set. The before-tax total of these items was five dollars. The knife set was actually for J's father, R, who would break the first knife he used and find the remaining knives so dull as to be useless.

J and M never gave each other anything, not directly, not even a greeting exchanged by means of D, though J did give D the cologne he used when he went to see M.

E gave R, who was her life partner, a pair of grey loafers that were identical to the pair he already owned but not worn on the outer heel, a foldable chair that R placed on their balcony and never used, and swimming trunks, goggles, and a membership to the local pool, which he hadn't used either. R eventually gave E his dollar-store knife set.

Finally, J, too, was able to stop seeing D, to whom she had given her love and whom she now loathed.

TIGRE

I was in your kitchen early this morning. The sun was rising and the birds were chirping. Only B was awake. His hair was curlier and lighter than usual, but his face looked the same. He was on the floor, squirting the cat with a water gun, and the cat was hissing at him. Later D woke up and ran around half-clothed in the half-light, opening the shutters, putting the kettle on the stove, feeding the cat. He nodded when he saw me and I nodded back. He got B ready for school and then the two of them left, one on the shoulders of the other. A long time passed before you emerged. You wore pink leg warmers, though it was hot. The sun was still rising. Your hair was in a knot and your eyes were almost closed. You went straight to the fridge without saying anything and poured yourself a bowl of cereal. When that was done, you had another. I was half-asleep so I didn't say anything either. I lay down in the corner and shut my eyes. I was on the sweet threshold of sleep when finally you spoke. You said it looked like a nice day, though the sun seemed to be perpetually rising so it was hard to tell. Maybe we can rent a cabin in the delta, you said, but I was sorry, I said, I was already in Tigre.

SUSHI AND I

We visit. Sushi positions herself beneath the shapes I make and tries
to sharpen her clawless paws. She meows until I scratch her head. If I
do a good job, she purrs. Excellent purr, I say, and pet her some more.
Throughout the day, Sushi directs me toward her food bowl. Though
she is capable of eating from it on her own, she finds the activity more
pleasurable when I am crouched beside her, rubbing her belly. When she
has finished eating, she lies on the cool kitchen tiles while I work nearby.
She stretches out on her back, belly up, limbs in the air. In the evening,
when she is spent from her time outdoors, lounging under the shade of the
neighbour's lawn chair, she climbs onto me. Excellent job, I tell her, when
she has situated her substantial girth in the middle of me, rotated twice,
and begun to knead my stomach. Keep up the good work, I say, for Sushi
is giving it her all. Soon she begins to purr and settles into the hollow she
has created, her nose next to mine. When I return to my book, however,
she promptly retreats to the farthest corner of the bed and wheezes loudly
before falling asleep.

EMOTIONAL SUPPORT PET

Stella picked up her small dog and a bag of rubbish. She took the elevator down nine floors, walked into the lobby, said hello to Juan, the doorman, who looked at her footwear, and exited the building. She went up to the big bin, which was surrounded by food waste, debris from construction sites, and leaf litter. She put down her rubbish, looked at it sternly, and said, Sit still, Facundo. Then she stepped on the lever to open the bin's lid, and tossed the dog inside.

STRANGE BEHAVIOUR IN DREAMS

You are not to blame. You were in another city, in another dream, when he dreamt his. During the brief period you lived next to him, you did not ever climb through the window into the bedroom of his dream. You did not ever contemplate touching that part of him, with that part of you, when you talked to him on the balcony you shared. You shared a language, too, which was not his first, or yours; not the language spoken in the country you were in, which was across the world from the country he had come from, and the country you had moved to. He moved into and out of the language you spoke to each other that night. You understood words for what could be touched or seen or pointed to on a map. But the words you didn't understand were mysterious abysses you leapt over or peered into, and now you see that so were your words, and that he fell into them and hasn't ever climbed out.

REASONS FOR STAYING

It had rained suddenly and the air was crisp. I was pleased and drunk.
We had eaten fruit soaked in wine and gone dancing. Only one of us
knew the steps. The other one of us followed them. Down and around
the ramparts to the old port. The lights were on by the sea. So many
more than I had ever seen. We stretched out in front of them. The waves
crashed and the fish flashed in netting and we were just getting started.
Why did you come and why do you stay, one of us laughed to the other.
I was the other. This had been the case for some time. I had an answer
or two prepared. Still, I was never sure it was the right one. I blamed the
sun-soaked days, on occasion his gaze, the sirens and cycles and birds in
flight, too often his plight, sweet melons, loudspeakers, the seekers, the
heat late one night. Tonight. Which was in fact becoming today. Still, we
played, just a little longer, until the sky was the colour of coral and it took
the last of our words away.

OUT OF REACH

We met between greys and mauves and we didn't look back. Not to
the webs we had woven of our pasts, not to the constellations that had
misguided us. We stocked up on rations and headed west.

These were long days over unwavering plains. We passed wheat fields and
grazing cows and stopped to snooze in the midday sun.

The entire sky was at our disposal.

Each night, we set up our blue tent below it. The tent was a little worse
for wear. It let in the wind and the rain. But also the stars. We gazed up
at them and fell asleep beneath them and woke floundering in birdsong.
We were not so good in the morning, but we came around.

On the other side of sleep, we'd root for foodstuffs in circles and squares
and cobble together a meal. Then we'd move along.

We were after the soundscapes, the half-light, the traces of flight. We
revelled in a good illusion. There was a certainty to those drawn-out days
of uncertainty; we talked around it, made loose and whimsical plans, but
never asked one another about it, never named it. We continued west.

What looked like clouds one morning were really mountains capped in
snow. It had been a long time since one of us had seen the snow. The other
one of us never had.

We found a trail up one of those mountains and waded through the clouds. Above them, one of us named what had always seemed out of speech.

The sun sank behind the other's voice. I see, they said, though they could not, for the sky had gone dark, and there was not a star in it.

SEEING STARS

I'll have you seeing stars, the one woman said, and the other woman did not know if this was a good thing or a bad one.

They were in a dark room, in a small cabin, in the sierras.

Outside, the wind blew and the sheep made noises. They sounded like humans trying to sound like sheep.

The one woman, who was an intense woman, had said these words very slowly and placed long spaces between them, and unable as she was to see this woman, the other woman couldn't tell what she had meant.

It was true that many people liked stars. People bought devices to magnify the stars and sat in cushy, reclining seats to observe the way some connected to others. Everybody liked a good shooting star.

But people also saw stars when they were punched by a comic-strip con, or during a fainting spell, or when the world whirled and they couldn't tell up from down. Most people didn't enjoy these things.

The other woman didn't think the one woman would wish these things upon her. She had come highly recommended. She had come wearing sandals and flowers and she had taken them all off.

Now, the other woman lay there in the dark, listening to the wind and the sheep, and waited for a clue.

I'll have you seeing stars, the one woman said again. If only you would let me.

The other woman was fairly sure she would not.

YOUNG FATHER, OTHER WOMAN

The other woman is in a club. She has soft white hair and pink skin.
She wears a polka-dot dress and carries a brown purse with a golden clasp.

She is dancing, wildly. Rays of green and purple light move across her
body and the dance floor.

A young father approaches her, coyly. He has dark hair and dull eyes and
wears a tight white shirt.

But the club is full, and to the other woman, this father is one of many:
she doesn't notice him, or doesn't show it.

The young father starts to dance with the other woman. He dances toward
her and then away from her and then in elaborate circles all around her.
Finally, he is dancing with her.

His head moves toward hers; his arms around hers; his legs between hers.
But they don't touch.

The music stops, and seconds later, they do, too. They look at each other.
Then the music starts again.

This new music has a different speed. They are slow to move their bodies
to it. When they do, some parts collide. That's okay, they don't say, and she
moves until she is away from him.

DANCE

You do not want to. You do not like to. You hope the singer will not
sing and the guitarist will not play. But suddenly, a bell is rung, and it
begins. Heads bob, toes tap. People at tables all around you get up to
dance. The person at your table gets up to dance. This person beckons
to you. Holds their hand out to you. Sways their hips and does pirouettes
before you. You are mortified. In your head you hear: There is no
escaping. Still, you look for a way out. A conga line forms. It comes your
way. Now other people beckon to you. There is no escaping, you hear
again, but you get off the chair and down on your knees and find that you
are crawling. You are crawling away from the music and toward the exit.
There are obstacles. High heels and chair legs. Waiters with wine bottles.
You avert them. You crawl your way through them and out the door.
When you are in the street, you stand up, brush the dirt off your knees,
and walk quickly into the night.

NIGHT GARDEN

The night was closed. I had not been asleep in it. I had been in the garden,
rooting around for mushrooms, suckles, cloves. The garden was thick with
blooms. There were leaves like brooms sweeping and fans whirring, others
like ears listening. I paid these no attention. I was at the edge. Beyond it,
the ocean was not pacific. It was frothing and sloshing; it had had a little
too much to drink. I wandered into this strange water, and the clouds
cleared a path to the lighthouse. Its beacon bled into the dawn. All around
it, birds responded in song. Fish with long snouts like saws and bells
for tails and translucent wings leapt into the air. The boats, ropes, and
buoys nodded, applauded. The day opened one colour at a time, magnolia,
apricot, lilac, in the hills, on the cliffs, in the thickets, hatches, yards, and
barns. I took the dusty road into the crux of it. Made a breakfast. Bumble
pie and cream whip. Water infused with linden, lemongrass. Then I went
back out to the garden. The early air was sweet and I hung my hammock
beneath the tree of sleep.

THE SECOND RULE

The first rule is sleep, second is foot, third is workout. First: second, most important rule: foot. Fuel. You are like an auto who needs to fill up before he drives. Without foot, you go nowhere fast. So ask yourself, where do you want to go? Maybe it is Ural Mountain Range. Maybe Rocky one. Maybe only upstairs, one flight or two flights of stairs. Take few minutes. Now you have answer, how you choose right foot? Process of eliminate. Until you have left right foot. Best foot. This foot makes you strong. Strength comes slowly. Takes many days, maybe years. First strength hard to notice. Second strength easier. You have skinny legs but all the while you are sleep, you are work out. Soon you bulk up. Still have belly because belly last to go. Then you see underneath strong abdominals. In centre most important part of being you are hard. Now can climb stairs, can climb mountains. Can twist and shout and shake all about.

EL MAGO

You go to see the wizard. He is not wearing a cape or holding a wand,
but he is dressed in tight white; he is wearing a funny hat. You leave your
shoes at the door. He inspects the top of you all the way to the bottom of
you. His right eye twitches; he does not approve. Still, he lets you into his
lair. It is full of yellow birds: toucans, cockatoos, canaries. The birds take
flight when you enter, then settle back down on perches that hang from
the ceiling, in cubbies in the wall, on his shoulders. On a large, bright
screen, scenes pass: green mounds rise from pixelated waters, women in
straw hats tend fields of inedible rice, blue and yellow fish swim through
two-dimensional reefs. Music is playing. Instruments made of wood.
Sounds meant to be coming from east of where you are. The wizard wants
to see you walk. What he sees is that you can't walk, not consistently.
So he adjusts you. One part of you, then another. He looks at the newly
adjusted you. Tells you to try it out. You skip and hop, pirouette. The birds
flutter in approval, but it is no good, you are not light on your feet. You
have not driven beyond the city's limits, past greengrocers and ice cream
parlours, fig trees and lemon trees, to visit this strange simulacrum of the
subtropics. You have come in order to leave upright, eyes on the horizon,
not on the floor. And though it's true there are some bright spots, some
lights you had not seen before, you still hobble back out the door.

BANDUNG

One night, we drive up into the clouds. When we reach the top of one hill, and then all the hills, we park and walk through the tea plantations. The land winds down in tidy rows and drops, finally, to a narrow path at the edge of the forest. Far below us, the city blinks, then goes out. We turn on our torches and follow the beams of light into the trees. The air is cool, but soon gusts of heat flow past us; fireflies flow past us; stars flow past us; and then we are surrounded by steam. Eventually, we reach a clearing in the forest. The clearing is full of laughter, but all we see is steam rising. We move close to each other but don't touch. Then the wind shifts, lifting the steam off a pool of black glass. A path of uneven stones leads down from the forest into the pool. Slippery stones we follow with one slow step, then another, until we shatter the glass. At first, the heat takes our breath away, but then we too begin to laugh. We burst into fits of laughter, hear great guffaws of laughter, as the steam settles around us.

DREAM OF THE SUBTROPICS

We were on vacation: white sand beaches, palm trees, the turquoise sea. What you'd expect. Only I didn't know where exactly—people were milling about in bright clothes, but they looked like us and I couldn't understand what the hell they were saying. I figured you might know, so I asked, and you answered in the language you spoke to that person you no longer see—you know the one—and of course I didn't understand.

Then we were at a restaurant having lunch—tables in the sand, fried fish, sugary drinks—and you recognized someone at the table next to us. She had shiny hair and large sunglasses. This woman was sitting with a child in a stroller, and you started talking to this child in that language, only you spoke in a baby voice. You hate it when people do that and I said so, but you just raised your baby voice.

Later we were at a nature reserve—it was all lush-like; there were large insects, loud birds, a couple of monkeys. Educational signs told the tourists about the different species—where they were from and what they ate and whatnot. You of course didn't care about the signs, you were busy taking hundreds of pictures you'll never look at again, but I did care and so I asked you what they said and you told me you didn't speak the local language.

At night we were in a room by the beach: it was a family-owned place, white clapboards, blue shutters, matching hammocks. We were in one of those hammocks; we could hear the ocean; we saw the occasional shooting star. You gasped each time, and the sounds you made weren't anything like the sounds you usually make, and I said, It's true the stars are brilliant but could you please stop, you're scaring me, and you just went on making them.

Later still, we were on that beach, sand in our hair, salt on our skin, inebriated, the complete cliché, and then we were having sex on the beach and you began to laugh the way people laugh in that language, so different from the laughter in our language. I asked what was so funny, I was not okay with your laughing during sex, and you just laughed louder and louder and finally you woke me up.

And so then we were not having sex and we were not on a beach. We were at home in bed and it was bloody cold. What's going on? I said, and I must have woken you up because you said, The dream of the subtropics again, and then you fell back into it and I of course didn't.

ABDUL AND I

I think I have a new friend.

Abdul.

We sit next to each other in French class.

We are beginners.

In French as in friendship.

Sometimes Abdul isn't there.
Then I sit next to Linda or Chan.
Linda is more advanced than Chan.

We practise a dialogue between
le pharmacien and madame.

Abdul is madame.

I wish she were me.

Madame has a sore throat.

She orders des pâtes
instead of des pastilles.

Le pharmacien does not know
what to do.

On break, he and madame
share a jambon sandwich.

It tastes not like pork
but like plastic.

After French class,
they walk to the subway.

Madame takes the orange line
and le pharmacien the green one.

Madame goes north to his French wife,
and le pharmacien east to his.

A FRIENDLY PERSON

Excuse me, by any ghost of a chance might you be a friendly person?

Not a false friend or another spectre.

A fellow spirit to chase after sundogs and sundry mirages.

Someone amenable to extended games of hide-and-seek and a hammock with good give.

Who is enthused by a good lagoon. A fine tree. A sandbank.

Who would go for a swim in an indigo stain left by the rain, or a sudden cascade, or a golden ribbon.

A person open to sanguine slips into unknown tongues and the occasional malapropism.

Who is liable to large helpings of bumble pie and fingerfuls of cream whip.

You will find, friendly person, that sometimes I eat too many questions. That I ask too much of food.

That I can be foolish. Shellfish. That I say the wrong sounds, though I pick the right words.

I vacillate, eternally. When I yawn, I do so strangely, wildly.

I amass trinkets of a pretty and practical nature. But I am lacking in living essentials: grooming supplies, kitchen implements, tools for the home.

I do what is my best. Lest you think otherwise.

What was that you said? You might not be. A friendly person. What about you over there? Or you in the red cap? By any ghost of a chance might you be friendly to this person?

RED CAPS AND PANT SUITS

He was surprised a little to find a friendly family in the club. The mother was taller and fuller than the father, who was a wisp of a man. Their three children, all boys, wore red caps and pant suits. The boys were dancing for money. Around poles. The tallest one, who was also the most beautiful, was a bad dancer. He had trouble finding the rhythm in the music and moving his body to it. The middle son was an enthusiastic dancer, which was contagious and why he earned the most money. The last son was plump and pear-shaped. He danced like no one was watching, as they say, though of course everyone was.

TONGS

People can choose the buns they want using tongs. Our selection of tongs is world-class. The red models are the most popular, regardless of the material they are made of, though black is also a favourite. After that, many people like beige and other skin-toned tongs. Our customers are free to use them as they please, so long as they do so to transport buns. Each day, we offer a wide variety of buns fresh from the oven. We have up to twenty kinds, in different shapes and sizes, from small through extra-large. Our customers are our priority, and we strive to ensure their buns are transported intact and in style.

THE BAKER

They have been doing construction since the summer.

Now there is a bakery next door.

Opening day.

Three days after opening day.

Serendipity: an unexpected and pleasant thing happens.

He asks me what I'm doing later.

Midnight (12 a.m.).

The movie finishes after midnight.

He doesn't push me to join him.

But I choose to stay until 4 in the morning.

He is a weak person in the morning.

Still, I start to have feelings for him.

Dalliance: a brief romantic relationship.

One fortnight (two weeks).

I decide to bury my feelings.

He is eight years younger than me.

I have not been able to forget what I felt for him.

Before I met him, there was not no one, but there was never someone.

Baking bread makes him sweat.

His bread is good. That's the truth.

SERIOUS CONSIDERATIONS

She would seriously consider going to the party, she said, if it was not too cold outside and if there was a vehicle involved. If there was no vehicle involved, she would still consider going, only not seriously. If it was too cold outside, she would not consider going at all, not even if there was a vehicle involved.

PINK TUTUS AND TIGHTS

Last night I went to a party. Everyone was dressed in pink tutus and tights. Exposed were the body parts people usually prefer to keep hidden—the men's bare thighs, the folds of fat in the women's stomachs—and so we all felt a little vulnerable. At first, we stared awkwardly at the different bodies, afraid to look each other in the eye. The waiters wore black tuxedos with cummerbunds and they carried out flutes of champagne on silver trays. When the band began to play, we moved to the dance floor. We danced alone or in small groups, allowing the waves of sound to wash through us. The champagne continued to flow and the ballerinas moved closer and closer together. Soon there was hardly any air between us, and the dance floor became a frothing sea of pink tutus.

PINK POISON

The rats are fighting again. It's the third time this week and I've had it. I go out into the lot next door and ask them to please lower their voices. Instead they squeal louder. I climb onto an old chair, its stuffing spilling out from the brown plastic seat. From up here, I see hundreds of rats run through abandoned furniture, leap into empty paint cans, climb up palm trees, and chase each other down ivy, their tails flailing. Branches break, fronds fall to the ground, dust rises into the air.

I'm going to call the police, I tell them, but they know it's an empty threat. Instead, I call a friend. She knows all about the rats next door. She herself has been next door. To ask the rats to quiet down. The friend brings pink poison. She ties the poison to gnarled roots and tree trunks and tucks it under rotten wooden shelves and a mouldy sofa. I get off the chair. We go inside and eat pizza. We have a pyjama party. That night, it thunderstorms.

The next day it rains loudly, and only in the evening, when the sun is setting, do the clouds clear. The sky turns bright pink. We go out into the lot. It's turned pink, too: the rain has streaked the poison across the pavement. On the sofa, up in the trees, under the shelves—everywhere we look—we see pink rats, though they are no longer fighting.

A BLUE HUMMINGBIRD

A blue hummingbird flew into my bedroom this morning. It flitted from fabric flower to fabric flower on my bedspread, but there was no nectar between the pink petals. An orange sun was setting over the sea on my computer screen, and the hummingbird flew toward it, then away from it, then toward it again, faster and faster toward the setting sun. It didn't stop when it got there; its beak shattered the screen and the sun disappeared. The hummingbird lay on its side on the floor, its tiny heart still heaving in a sea of colourless glass.

SUGAR ISLAND

I'll meet you on the island, he said, but she didn't know which island, or when.

Sometime later, she understood he was on an island of sugar, staying in a small hotel with a fruit garden.

She looked for the garden and found a man rocking in it, among bluebottles and hummingbirds. Good afternoon, she said to the man. He's gone fishing, the man said to her.

She walked to the beach. It was split in two by a river of molasses. Along the river's banks, sugar slipped slowly underwater.

He stood back where it all began. Hello, she smiled. Hi, she waved. But he looked straight through her before sifting slowly into the forest.

Overhead, clouds closed up the sky. The beach filled with mist. Now she could not tell which way was the forest and which was the sea.

She chose the sea. She sat down in it and the waves washed through her and the sugar shifted under her.

Two lovebirds dropped down from the clouds. This way, they seemed to say, and she lifted herself up and followed them into the forest.

The forest was many greens and browns: mint, cinnamon, and star anise. She walked along the river. Listless leaves dripped into the caramel water.

She found him in his nook. Saccharine smoke rose in wafts and wisps around him. Hello, he whistled. It's nice to see you, I wish I could stay.

Hanging from a hook were bright fish with sequined eyes. Now the only trace of him was scales like lace on the forest floor.

She put a fish on the fire. It crackled as its flesh curled in the flames. The wind shifted and the smoke took to boughs and bellows, rose in rows around blossoms and leaves. It carried him back to her. Stop this trickery! she said. But he was fickle, wicked.

She had erred on the side of words instead of actions. She had been duped. He had not meant what he had said but what he had not done, where he had not been.

Still, she kept after him for some time. She followed the island's movements, its cycles of colour, its cloudscapes. She took the river past the falls to where she'd heard him hum. The sun slumbered. Mangroves fed on painted snails. She found a bent-up old lawn chair, and his sneakers and yellow shirt, scattered in the sand.

She left those behind her. Granulated clouds hung from one end of the island, then the other. Parrots like pink frosting flew up and crossed the sky. The sea set pearls and coral in it.

YOU, DOWN ON THE BEACH

I think that was the first experience losing something from my heart. At first I didn't want to let it go, so I held on tightly. But the more I clung to it, the more it desired to be free of me. It tried to escape but I held on tighter still, until one day, when I wasn't looking, it succeeded and was gone. First I searched for it in all the usual places, like in my coat pockets and between the cushions on the couch. Next I looked in unusual places: in the oven, then mixed in with the cat chow, in my belly button, even.

Weeks—or was it months?—passed before I felt ready to look outside. I raised the blinds and peered through one window, then the next. It was a blue day, cold and bright. I opened the front door and stepped onto the lawn. The lawn was overgrown. It sloped slowly upward to the evergreen tree, your evergreen tree. It was taller than our house now, my house now. I started to climb it to see what I could see from the very top. I climbed carefully, looking for the best place to put a foot and then a hand. As I got higher, I started to feel the sea, and when I reached the top, I sat down on a branch that sank and swam in the wind. I could see the whole town, the white houses and orange roofs, and beyond them the shore. I could see the surface of the water shifting in the wind, and the gulls drifting. For some time, I sat there, looking at the top of the town and the ocean. Then, suddenly, I thought I saw you down on the beach, and I gasped. You were standing just beyond the wooden boats, in your red parka. But parts of you were bigger than I remembered, and others were smaller, and finally I wasn't sure if I had found you, or imagined you in someone else, or if I hadn't seen anyone at all.

CARMELO

We lie down on the beach and float in and out of the heat. In the treetops above us, and the branches hanging down around us, the cicadas are playing. A few begin, then the others join them. They know one song and they keep on singing it. We drift here for hours, listening to them play. The sun slowly moves us out of the shade and we decide to play too. We slip out of our clothes and into the stream. The water is warm and soft, and soon we are asleep in it. When we wake, we are swaying below the surface. A big silver fish swims past and we follow it through rays of light and forests of algae. We see a turtle. It snaps at the fish, or at us, and bubbles float up from its mouth. The fish leads us to the shallows on the other side. We sit up in the sand and poke our heads into the heat. There is less of it now. The sun is lower in the sky, and when it finally sinks behind the trees, a breeze comes over from the sea. It moves the branches and leaves, and all the cicadas in all the trees play louder and tighter until the sun is song.

J THE K

He lived his whole life at the bottom of my heart. He had been my kinesiologist and then my boyfriend. It is okay to have a crush on your healer, said a friend like a gem. It is the closeness to goodness.

But in the end it was not okay. What was the weight of that disappointment?

I was still getting to unknow him when he moved in with his new girlfriend, who became his wife, and they started a family together. They made a girl they named after a famous singer, and two years later, a boy. His name they made up.

They were good in love. They painted the kids' room yellow and renovated the basement. Then they built a sunroom.

The construction workers were there half the summer that year and the noise nearly drove me out of my mind. I went for long walks through the city. Everyone had left it for the lakes or woods.

One weekend, they left too, and the house filled with a silence that was sweet, then saccharine.

I thought I might be sick. I went to bed and did not leave.

I tried to read. I picked up one book, then another, but my mind wouldn't stay with the words for long. It went to the other words, the ones I had to tell him. A perpetual state, the rehearsing of them. If only he would take them from me, I thought, I would be cured. But he would not. He was always running about, putting the kids down, picking them up; the moment was never opportune. So I kept at this conversation that could not begin and could not end.

The kids grew. The house expanded and shrunk. The colours of life changed. But the bandage remained: the words I could never tear off.

THE SAME DREAM

They had been driving alone at night, on a
highway through the desert. All around them
stars fell from the sky and landed softly in the
sand. Then there was a man dressed in black,
and she gasped, as though they'd crashed, and
their bodies jolted forward in unison. They
opened their eyes wild in her bed, their hearts
pounding, the siren sounding, the blue light
flashing up from the street below.

A DIFFICULT WEEK

It was a difficult week for the illness. It had had to fight hard, for many hours each day, and didn't get much rest. But it was tenacious and had excellent reserves of energy, and finally, it won the battle. Now, Schmitt was dead.

THOSE PROBLEMS

The ocean can help you forget those problems: problems with your spouse or your life partner; problems with your boss at the office, or problems because you don't have an office; problems seeing objects from a distance or from up close; problems with your skin such as adult-onset acne or varicose veins; relationship problems because you have a boyfriend who looks at your friends while you're looking at him; health problems because you weigh too much or too little; problems when you try to fall asleep or when you try to have sex; problems with your addiction to cigarettes, or to coffee, or to refined sugar; problems because you are stressed, or depressed, or anxious; and other problems too.

The ocean has already helped many people with their problems. They go to wherever the earth ends and the water begins and they sit in the sand or on top of a cliff or on a bench overlooking the waves. They don't look like they are doing much, and neither will you, but they are letting the ocean carry away their problems on the crest of a wave or on the shoulders of a humpback whale. They may have spotted a sand crab to bury their problems in a dark tunnel below the beach, or a seashell so their problems can wind round and round the hollow home of a snail lost at sea. If your problems are many, you might consider feeding them to a school of rainbow fish, or if you've just one problem, and it's a big one, you could let a shark feast on it for supper.

NOTES

For some things that are required of you (and more!), see John Ashbery's *Flow Chart*.

Was rest ultimately assured? Erin can say.

"Franklin has a tremendous will to live": observation my brother's.

The bell that tolls in Ms. Stella Maris Echevarria's left ear, the indigo stain left by the rain, and the tree of sleep are Guadalupe Dueñas's images, my words.

La noche era cerrada in Agustina Bazterrica's novel *The Unworthy* before it opened in "Night Garden."

El Mago's birds are migratory: they spend part of the year in Tomás Downey's story "Hombrecito."

Abdul, Linda, Chan, and Rubie Tuesday, the friend like a gem, studied French together. Abdul and Rubie Tuesday's dialogue was spoken in one version in class, in French, then in *Strange Water*, in English.

I found the bent-up old lawn chair in a Stuart Ross poem and put it in Sugar Island.

ACKNOWLEDGEMENTS

Thank you to my wonderful and amusing family and friends, whose words and ways are afloat throughout *Strange Water*, whether they know it or not. (Only the good ones!—The good words and ways, by which I mean the strange ones; not the good family and friends.)

To the authors I have translated, some of whom figure in the aforementioned group, for same.

Thanks, especially, to Tomás Downey, who figures in both groups, for reading an earlier version with a stranger name.

And to Stuart Ross, who does too, for the special attention he has always given to my words and to the words of others.

To Javier, whose words are not in this book, but who is in it in numerous other ways.

PREVIOUS APPEARANCES

Earlier versions and Spanish versions of some of these fictions have been published in *Círculo de Poesía, dusie, EVENT Magazine, Litro, Northern Testicle Review, periodicities,* and *Slice Magazine,* and by above/ground press, Proper Tales Press, and Socios Fundadores.

SARAH MOSES is a Canadian writer and literary translator from Spanish and French. Her translations include *Tender Is the Flesh*, by Agustina Bazterrica, and *Die, My Love*, by Ariana Harwicz, which was longlisted for the International Booker Prize and shortlisted for the Republic of Consciousness Prize, the Premio Valle Inclán, and the Best Translated Book Award. With Tomás Downey, she co-translated *Sos una sola persona*, a selection of poems by Stuart Ross. Forthcoming publications include a co-translation of Julio Cortázar's letters with Anne McLean (Archipelago Books) and *The Place Where Birds Die*, stories by Tomás Downey (Invisible Publishing). Sarah has written one chapbook of fictions in Spanish, *as they say*, and one in English, *Those Problems*. *Strange Water* is her first full-length collection. She lives in Buenos Aires and Toronto, where she's from.

ALSO BY SARAH MOSES

Chapbooks
as they say (Socios Fundadores, 2016)
Those Problems (Proper Tales Press, 2016)

Book-Length Translations
Rocío Araya, *Head in the Clouds* (Elsewhere Editions, 2024)
Agustina Bazterrica, *Nineteen Claws and a Black Bird* (Pushkin Press/
    Scribner, 2023)
Fernand Deligny, *Camering: Fernand Deligny on Cinema and the Image*
    (ed. Marlon Miguel, Leiden University Press, 2022)
Paula Rodríguez, *Urgent Matters* (Pushkin Press, 2022)
Agustina Bazterrica, *Tender Is the Flesh* (Pushkin Press/Scribner, 2020)
Stuart Ross, *Sos una sola persona* (co-translated w/ Tomás Downey,
    Socios Fundadores, 2020)
Ariana Harwicz, *Die, My Love* (Charco Press, 2017)

ABOUT 1366 BOOKS

1366 Books is an imprint of Guernica Editions, launched in 2024 to bring to light two books of innovative but accessible fiction annually. Each title—whether a novel, stories, or microfictions—is a unique literary experience. Imprint editor Stuart Ross welcomes submissions of manuscripts that challenge or work to redefine the boundaries of the genre. He is especially interested in seeing manuscripts of experimental fiction from members of diverse and marginalized communities. Write to Stuart at 1366books@gmail.com.

2024
The Apple in the Orchard, by Brian Dedora
Strange Water, by Sarah Moses

Exploding Fictions

MIX
Paper
FSC® C100212

Printed by Imprimerie Gauvin
Gatineau, Québec